Also by the Author

The Bookman's Tale

First Impressions

The Further Adventures

of Ebenezer Scrooge

Charlie Lovett

VIKING

VIKING

An imprint of Penguin Random House LLC

375 Hudson Street

New York, New York 10014

penguin.com

ISBN: 978-0-52542-910-4

Printed in the United States of America

1   3   5   7   9   10   8   6   4   2

Set in LTC Kennerley Pro
Designed by Alissa Rose Theodor

To Mim
Who showed me how to keep Christmas
And to Lucy & Jordan
For whom it has been a joy to keep

Christmas isn't just a day; it's a frame of mind.

—VALENTINE DAVIES

Contents

Preface

It seems that Charles Dickens always loved Christmas. He wrote essays, stories, and scenes in his novels dealing with various aspects of the holiday from early in his career until shortly before his death. But in 1843, he did something different—he created a philosophy of Christmas in what would become his most enduring and popular single work, the novella *A Christmas Carol*. Dickens wrote this tale in just six weeks, beginning in September, and presented it to the world on December 19. By Christmas Eve, the first edition of six thousand copies had sold out.

Just a few paragraphs into the story, Scrooge's nephew Freddie remarks that to him Christmas has always been

> *a good time; a kind, forgiving, charitable, pleasant time; the only time I know of, in the long calendar of the year, when men and women seem by one consent to open their shut-up hearts freely, and to think of people below them as if they really were fellow-passengers to the grave, and not another race of creatures bound on other journeys.*

Dickens described this idea as the "Carol Philosophy" of Christmas, and to many of us it continues to sum up the way we feel about the holiday season. The philosophy played out in the life of Charles Dickens, through both his continued literary attention to Christmas and his concern for social reform. But how did the Carol Philosophy resonate in the life of Ebenezer Scrooge after that fateful Christmas of 1843? At the end of Stave IV of *A Christmas Carol*, Scrooge vows to "honour Christmas in my heart, and try to keep it all the year." So perhaps it is fitting to turn to the Scrooge of 1863 for a little lesson on keeping Christmas.

The Further Adventures

of Ebenezer Scrooge

Marley's Ghost

S crooge was alive, to begin with. There could be no doubt whatever about that—alive and kicking. Not that I know why that particular verb should exemplify life; for Scrooge's part it might better be said that he was alive and singing, or alive and laughing, or alive and generally making a nuisance of himself.

Yes, though Scrooge had approached, then reached, and finally surpassed the age at which most of us, in particular his former partner, Jacob Marley, like Hamlet and his unhappy clan, "shuffle off this mortal coil," he nonetheless lived on, with no noticeable diminution of energy, or ecstasy, or enthusiasm. Cratchit knew this well. How could it be otherwise? Scrooge and Cratchit had been partners for nigh on twenty years and in all that time Cratchit, though he had watched as the lines of age had waged their admittedly only modestly successful assault on Scrooge's visage, had noted no decrease in his partner's liveliness. Which brings me back to the point I started from. There is no doubt that Scrooge was as alive as ever—some might say more alive.

Oh, but he was an openhanded benefactor, Scrooge! A generous, charitable, jolly, gleeful, munificent old fool, yielding as a feather pillow that welcomed the weariest soul to its downy breast. The light within him melted his hardened features, reddened his nose, puffed out his cheeks, loosened his gait (as well as his purse strings), made his eyes sparkle and his lips glow, and bubbled forth in his dulcet voice. A tuneful rhyme was ever in his throat, and his frosty eyebrows fooled no one. He carried his own warmth always about him; he could thaw ice blocks with his presence as easily at Christmastide as in the dog days of summer.

External heat and cold had little influence on Scrooge—no summer swelter could dissuade his glee nor winter weather chill his cheery countenance. No breeze that swayed the grasses of spring was gentler than he, no falling snow more soft and soothing, no rain more apt to nurture. And like the rain and snow and hail and sleet and beating sun combined, like our own relentless English weather, Scrooge never stopped, never altered that perfect disposition—not to please himself, and certainly not to please those inhabitants of London on whom his constant kindnesses had grown wearisome from years of use.

Nobody ever stopped in the street to say, with gladsome looks, "My dear Mr. Scrooge, how are you? When will you come to see me?" For they knew that come he would, and bring gifts to the children he would, and press a coin into each of their outstretched hands he would, and sing a pleasant song he would, and such unrelenting happiness would he bring that the household would find it difficult to bear. No beggars implored him to bestow a trifle, for a ten-pound note would end their careers. No children asked him what was the o'clock, having no time to spare for stories and songs and tossing upon the knee. Even the blind men's dogs appeared to know him, and when they saw him coming on, they would tug their owners into doorways and up courts; for where would such dogs be once Scrooge laid eyes upon their masters—Scrooge, who would gladly lead a blind man to Dover, if that were his destination? No, the dogs would wag their tails and hide their masters until Scrooge had passed, their employment ensured for another day.

But what did Scrooge care? There was always another blind man or beggar or child just round the corner, always room in the crowded paths of life for his bottomless well of human sympathy.

Once upon a time—of all the days in the year, that longest day when shadows in the narrowest alleys do not lengthen until well past the hour when men like Scrooge have taken their evening meal—old Scrooge whistled his way down a narrow street of Westminster. It was hot, sultry, sweaty weather and the shimmer on the Thames was enough to cloud the mind of the most clear-thinking man. The city clocks had just gone three, but the sun seemed disinclined to rest in its glaring pursuit of those souls who slogged along the paving stones. The heat came pouring in at every chink and keyhole and spared no one, from the lowliest clerk to the wealthiest miser who ever captained a countinghouse.

In a government office in Whitehall, labouring to keep a certain column of numbers from encroaching upon another, similar column and thus bringing down the empire, sat Scrooge's nephew, Freddie, and as he had left his door standing open, in the vain hope that some stirring of the air might bring a hint of relief from the stifling heat, he had not the turn of the handle to warn him of his uncle's approach.

"A Merry Christmas, nephew! God save you!" cried Scrooge in a cheerful voice.

"Christmas?" replied the startled nephew. "I've no time now for Christmas, uncle."

Scrooge inexplicably wore a muffler wound round his

ruddy neck, and this he now unwound in a leisurely fashion, as if it were one and the same to him whether it adorned him or not. His eyes sparkled as he endured the impatient stare of his nephew.

"No time for Christmas!" said Scrooge. "You don't mean that, I am sure."

"I do," said Freddie. "Merry Christmas on the longest day of summer? What right have you to be merry, when all around you are working? What reason have you to be merry? You're poor enough."

"Come, then," replied Scrooge gaily. "What right have you to be dismal? What reason have you to be morose?"

"Not this again, uncle," said Freddie.

"I'm poor because I choose to be, because I take more pleasure in giving away my gold than in hoarding it to pay for my meagre needs," answered Scrooge, ignoring his nephew. "And so I say again, Merry Christmas."

Fearing that his superior, the assistant to the undersecretary of a governmental department the purpose of which Scrooge had never entirely understood, might overhear their conversation, Freddie pulled shut the connecting door and lowered his voice. "It is all the same to me, uncle, if you wish me a Merry Christmas on every day of the year. I've no objection if you keep Christmas in your way; but there are others who say that Bedlam is the place for a fool who walks about with 'Merry Christmas' on his lips on the hottest days of summer. There are those who mutter behind your back that such an idiot as Scrooge should be stuffed like a goose, wrapped in mistletoe, and floated across the Thames."

"Nephew," replied his uncle gently, "why should Christmas be the only good time of the year, the only kind, forgiving, charitable, pleasant time? Why should Christmas be the only time when men and women open their shut-up hearts freely and think of people below them as if they really were fellow passengers to the grave?"

"Your sentiments are admirable, uncle, I have no doubt, but I have bills to pay and books to balance. I'm a year older than last summer and not a farthing richer, though of all the quantities that surround me—my wife's allowance, my children's appetites, my haberdasher's bill—the only one which seems never to increase is my bank balance. I should love to have your leisure for cheerfulness, uncle, but most of us"—and here he glanced at the closed door which hid his superior—"can afford no more than a few days of 'Merry Christmas.'"

"I shall come to dine with you, tomorrow," said Scrooge, paying no more mind to his nephew's speech than a duck to a raindrop.

"We've little to spare, uncle."

"And little is exactly what I require. Good works, kindness, my cheerful Christmas greetings that you so abhor—these are enough to fill me." Scrooge retrieved his muffler from his nephew's desk and twirled it in the air about his head. Then, with a twinkle in his eye, he pulled open the door to the assistant to the undersecretary's office and bellowed, "Merry Christmas!" to that bureaucratic soul. And as his nephew tried in vain to quiet the old man, Scrooge skipped back into the street with a hearty "And a Happy New Year," and was soon gone from view.

An hour later, rounding the corner of Threadneedle Street, Scrooge caught sight of two gentlemen approaching. They were dressed in black from the glossy leather on the tips of their boots to the shiny silk at the tops of their hats. One swung a silver-handled walking stick in his right hand; the other, an identical stick in his left. In bearing they reminded Scrooge of nothing less than the figurehead on the prow of some ancient sailing ship—chests thrust proudly forward, they glided down the street towards him. In another moment they were upon him and Scrooge burst forth with a hearty "Merry Christmas."

"Have I the honour of addressing Mr. Pleasant or Mr. Portly?" asked Scrooge, for, you see, as both men were pleas-ant and portly, and as Scrooge could not, for his life, recall their surnames, he generally addressed the pair (and they were always seen as a pair) as the Messrs. Pleasant and Portly.

"Mr. Scrooge," replied Mr. Portly (if it was not Mr. Pleasant), "it is fortuitous that we should meet."

"Fortuitous indeed," added Mr. Pleasant (if it was not Mr. Portly), who seemed almost to mouth the words that emerged from his companion's lips. "We should very much like to confer with you, Mr. Scrooge. I am afraid your munificence is, once again, at odds with your account at the bank."

"Yes, your account," said Mr. Portly, reaching into a folio that he carried and presenting three cheques that bore the flourish with which Mr. Scrooge endorsed his generosity.

"You see, Mr. Scrooge," said Mr. Pleasant, pulling a sheet of figures from the depths of a pocket, "your current balance is exactly . . ." He ran his finger down the column of numbers, but before it reached the bottom Mr. Portly interrupted.

"Twopence. Which is not quite enough to cover these cheques. Fifty pounds to the Society for the Relief of Distress. Forty pounds for the . . ." And here Mr. Portly squinted, hesitating just long enough for Mr. Pleasant to continue.

"For the Metropolitan Sanitary Association. One hundred pounds for the Home for Deserted Destitute Children."

"Your largesse," continued Mr. Portly, "though well intentioned, is not well supported by your means, Mr. Scrooge."

"Liberality, my good gentlemen, liberality," responded Scrooge with his usual tone of good cheer. It was a word that brought a frown to the face of Mr. Portly and caused Mr. Pleasant to shake his head.

"Liberality is not the business of a bank," said Mr. Pleasant, who was beginning to look distinctly undeserving of his sobriquet.

"Mankind should be your business," said Scrooge with a smile. "The common welfare should be your business; charity, mercy, forbearance, and benevolence should all be your business."

"Surely," said Mr. Portly, "there are those who rightly make such things their business. There are charities and philanthropists all over London. The bank is a different sort of institution."

"You of all people should know that, Mr. Scrooge," said Mr. Pleasant.

"Indeed," added Mr. Portly, "there was a time when few in London understood the business of finance better than yourself."

Scrooge paid little attention to this allusion to his pecunious past, but instead returned to the theme he had attempted to introduce at the beginning of the conversation.

"You do not seem to have a Merry Christmas in your hearts,

gentlemen. If you would but remember that festive season of the year, you would certainly admit that we should make some slight provision for the poor and destitute."

"We do make ourselves merry at Christmas, and at that time we do make such provisions, to be sure," said Mr. Portly.

"But we can hardly afford," concluded Mr. Pleasant, "to make idle people merry all the year round."

"Can't you?" asked Scrooge with a knowing wink, to which the bankers responded only with a mutual shrug. Seeing clearly that it would be useless to pursue his point, Scrooge made a slight bow to the two gentlemen and betook himself down the street in the general direction of his place of business. When Mr. Portly waved the three offending cheques in the air and cried at the retreating figure, "But, Mr. Scrooge, your account!" Scrooge could only be heard wishing "Merry Christmas"—not so much to the two bankers as to the general populace.

Let us consider Scrooge as he recedes into the unremitting glare of the summer sun. He seems a living oxymoron. Once a wealthy man who dressed in a pauper's threadbare black, he can now count twopence to his name yet wears a waistcoat embroidered in such exquisite colours that, were it not for his strange behaviour, one might take him for some lord or baron. There are those who mistake him, in his festive attire, for a well-known writer, a certain Mr. Dickens, who is known for his eccentricities of dress, and were Scrooge's hair a bit less white and his beard a bit more full the resemblance would have been close enough to fool any casual observer. On closer inspection, however, we find that Scrooge's attire, though festive, is distinctly out of date, and shows such signs of wear as might be seen in the garb of one whose riches are but a distant memory.

The heat and the haze thickened so, people slowed their gait to a near crawl as they made their way through the streets. Gentlemen carried hats only to fan their florid faces; ladies were not seen about at all. Newsboys sought out what slivers of shadow the cruel sun had overlooked; horses dreamed of crisp air and open spaces and pawed at the ground as if it might contain some hidden well of coolness. The ancient tower of a church became all but invisible in the grimy haze and when its old bell struck the hours and the quarters, the sound was muffled by the very air, as if someone had wrapped a cloak about the clapper.

The offices of Scrooge and Cratchit were in an altogether less savoury area of London than the bank of Messrs. Pleasant and Portly—a neighbourhood where the streets and doorways were narrow, where the "finery" of the local inhabitants was more likely to consist of rags than of silk, and where the stench of humanity, ripened by the harsh summer sun, was such that decency prohibits describing it. Here, in the larger of two rooms—the smaller being really no more than a cupboard—Bob Cratchit toiled away. Sometimes people new to London called Cratchit Scrooge, a misappellation that invariably caused amusement amongst the neighbours (for the firm was located on a street so narrow that its tenants enjoyed few secrets). Anyone who had lived in the neighbourhood for more than a fortnight, even if he had not met Scrooge, knew of him, and no one who knew of him could possibly mistake the one partner, grimly adding and subtracting figures with barely a mutter and with a brow as tightly knit as the weave of the finest cloth on Savile Row, for the other.

The other—that is, Ebenezer Scrooge—made his way briskly through the streets, scattering crowds of workers bound from their stifling offices to their stifling lodgings with his regular shouts of "Merry Christmas!" punctuated occasionally by an equally inappropriate "And a Happy New Year!" When one unsuspecting clerk stopped Scrooge to enquire about this odd greeting, the New Year being, in the mind of the clerk, some six months distant, Scrooge replied that the calendar was an arbitrary governor of a man's life and that the year began anew whenever one decided to live his life in a new way. The clerk managed to escape before Scrooge could explain just how this change might be effected, but his disappearance made not the slightest difference in Scrooge's holiday temper. Only a few steps on, he paused before the open door of an office to regale the occupants with a Christmas carol, but at the first sound of

"*God Bless you merry, gentlemen!*
May nothing you dismay"

the door was slammed with such energy of action that even Scrooge came close to flinching before he toddled off down the road.

Just as the hour for shutting up the countinghouse arrived, so did Scrooge, strolling through the open door with his usual goodwill.

"You should take the day off tomorrow," he said, as Cratchit dismounted from his stool. "Spend some time with your little grandson. I'm sure young Timothy would find it quite convenient."

"I don't find it convenient," replied Cratchit in the tone of a parent attempting for the hundredth time to disabuse a stubborn child of a ridiculous notion. "And I don't find it fair. If I did such a thing and failed to reduce my salary by half a crown, I'd think the firm ill-used."

"And yet," said Scrooge, "you don't think the firm ill-used when I draw a day's wages for an hour's copying letters and seven more wandering about the city wishing strangers a merry Christmas."

Cratchit observed that, whilst this was a bit unfair, it happened only about once a week.

"A poor excuse for picking your pocket," said Scrooge. "If it eases your conscience, you may come in all the earlier the next day."

Cratchit remarked that he would be of little help to his grandson if he were not careful to see the firm remained profitable and that he fully intended to arrive at an early hour the next morning; he flinched only moderately when, as he left, Scrooge bellowed after him, "Merry Christmas!" Cratchit, after all, was used to it.

The office was closed in a moment, and Scrooge walked with a lightness in his step, puzzling to other pedestrians weighed down by the heat, to a nearby tavern. There he settled in to read the papers and to take his evening meal in a room which anyone else on such a day would have called stuffy but which Scrooge thought of as cosy. The tavern keeper had learned long ago that whatever Scrooge took for dinner (tonight it was mutton), he would take Christmas pudding with it, and so that concoction had been prepared in anticipation of Scrooge's arrival. The tavern keeper knew, too, that although Scrooge could rarely afford to pay his bill (tonight was no exception), he was nonetheless good for business; most of London knew that Scrooge dined at this particular tavern, and much of London stopped by now and again for a mug of ale and a chance to gawk at the old fool daintily consuming his Christmas pudding in the long days of summer.

Recall, if you will, Scrooge's lodgings—the lowering pile of a building huddled in the dark corner of a dark yard amongst neighbours which would have seemed decrepit on their own but which, by comparison to the house where Scrooge made his abode, positively gleamed with youth. At the front of the house we find the heavy door with its great knocker, behind that door the flight of stairs wide enough to accommodate a hearse broadside, and at the top of those stairs Scrooge's gloomy suite of rooms: sitting room, bedroom, and lumber room, none furnished with any chattels beyond the necessary. Some things about Scrooge had remained unchanged after his well-publicised transformation two decades ago, amongst them his ascetic domestic arrangements.

The sole exception to this rule stood by the window in the sitting room. Scrooge called it his "German toy," but to those who glimpsed it from the street below it was merely a Christmas tree. Even in the pale evening light it sparkled and glittered with bright objects. There were miniature French-polished tables, chairs, bedsteads, and various other articles of domestic furniture (wonderfully made, in tin, at Wolverhampton) perched amongst the boughs; there were jolly broad-faced little men, much more agreeable in appearance than many real men—and no wonder, for their heads came off and showed them to be full of sugarplums; there were fiddles and drums; there were tambourines, books, workboxes, paint boxes, and sweetmeat boxes; there was real fruit, made artificially dazzling with gold leaf; there were imitation apples, pears, and walnuts, crammed with surprises; in short, as a child visitor to Scrooge's rooms once delightedly whispered to her bosom friend, "There is everything, and more."

In what most of London had come to think of as his former life (that is, the time before the appearance of four ghosts one Christmas Eve transformed his general outlook), Scrooge had derived a substantial augmentation to his income by letting out the other rooms in the building as offices. As then, those rooms were now filled in the daytime with clerks and visited by gentlemen who resembled, in clothing and carriage, the Messrs. Pleasant and Portly; however, Scrooge's income from all this bustling activity could now be expressed in a single syllable: nil. The rooms were now let, on terms that far exceeded liberal, to various charitable societies which attempted, in their various ways, to fulfill the various needs of London's lowermost classes.

By the time Scrooge returned to the house, the windows were all dark and even the yard was deep in shadow, for the sun had finally been coaxed out of the sky into its briefest retirement of the year. Now, it is a fact that there was nothing at all particular about the knocker on the door, except that, as aforementioned, it was very large. Nonetheless, it was Scrooge's habit, having his key in the lock, to look deep into the shadows that rippled across the surface of the brass. A passing observer might have attributed this behaviour to the acknowledged fact that Scrooge had as much of what is called "fancy" about him as any man in London—including the wittiest actor in the West End and the happiest lunatic in Bedlam. But to Scrooge, the behaviour of the knocker had become an omen, a harbinger of what might await him in his rooms above. On this night, as on many previous nights in the past twenty years, Scrooge saw in the knocker, without its undergoing any intermediate process of change, not a knocker, but Marley's face.

Yes, Jacob Marley, once partner in Scrooge's countinghouse but now dead one score and seven years, was in the habit of making periodic appearances in Scrooge's knocker. Tonight his countenance glowed lurid in the evening haze, as if the sun had not undertaken its brief nocturnal sojourn but still reflected off the polished brass. To anyone else, it would have seemed horrible, but in Scrooge, who knew what the ghostly spectacles and curiously stirred hair portended, Marley's appearance engendered not fear but delight. Scrooge rubbed the knocker, which was once again merely a knocker, with one hand as he turned the key with the other. Chuckling, he entered the dim hall and mounted the stairs, trimming his candle as he went.

Even at that time of year, when the yard without was never truly dark, half a dozen gas lamps out of the street wouldn't have lighted the entry too well, so you may suppose it was pretty dark even with Scrooge's candle.

Up Scrooge bounced, not caring a button for that: Darkness was cheap, and a penny saved in tolerating darkness for himself might subsequently be spent providing light for someone else. As soon as he passed through his door, he eagerly searched his rooms for any evidence that the event foreshadowed in the knocker had already taken place, but found everything in its usual order and himself quite alone. The door to his rooms he left unlocked, as if this would provide a more convenient ingress for his expected visitor. Quite satisfied with this minimal and wholly unnecessary preparation, he took off his cravat and put on his dressing gown and slippers, eschewing his nightcap in silent sympathy with the rest of London, who, unlike him, suffered from the heat. He sat down before the grate—empty as much because of economy as because of the weather—to read a novel by the flickering light of his taper.

At the end of a chapter in which the youthful hero had walked from London to Dover with little to assuage his hunger or protect him from the elements, Scrooge laid his book upon the table so that he might wipe a tear from his eye, so moved was he by the plight of the fictional boy. He gazed for a moment at the tiles around his fireplace, barely visible in the candlelight. They were designed to illustrate the Scriptures, but Scrooge had come to think of them as unnecessarily focused on violent incidents from the Old Testament. He had, the previous year, thought to replace them with a more fanciful set by an artist whose work he had seen at an exhibition, but on his way to visit the artist he had emptied his pockets to a destitute woman he met in the street (Scrooge often travelled by such streets as were likely to introduce him to such women) and so, having not a farthing with which to commission a fresh set of tiles, he had turned his wanderings in another direction, arriving home without having sought out the artist after all.

Finding the tiles difficult to focus on in the dimness, Scrooge turned his attention to the one object in the room (besides, some would say, the Christmas tree) that might seem superfluous—a bell pull that hung in the sitting room and communicated for some purpose long forgotten with a chamber in the highest storey of the building. Rising from his chair, he grasped the pull and gently tugged it, knowing that more than the most tentative pressure would surely end what had been an extraordinarily long life for the threadbare pull. At first, the bell scarcely made a sound, but soon it rang loudly, and as if in sympathy, so did every bell in the house.

"Come along, friend," cried Scrooge, "show yourself! I've no wish to sit up all night, even on so short a night as this."

Straightaway a clanking began as heavy chains were dragged up the stairs. Satisfied that the bells had done their work, Scrooge settled back into his chair and waited for the arrival of the ghost (for it was none other than Marley's ghost who dragged chains ever closer to Scrooge's apartment). Scrooge had considered Marley no more than a business partner in life; he had come to think of Marley as his dear friend in death and had even taken to calling him by his given name. It was this name he uttered when a momentary flame leapt up in the grate, signaling the ghost's arrival at his door.

"Don't keep a poor old man waiting, Jacob!" he cried with delighted anticipation. "Come in and take a seat." Scrooge could never say exactly how Marley did come in—he did not float through the door nor seep under it nor ooze through the keyhole. One moment he was rattling his chains on the landing, and the next he was sitting in the chair opposite Scrooge, his boots propped up on the fender. The phantom brought with him a blast of chill air which would have been welcomed by anyone else in London that night but which had no more effect on Scrooge than the afternoon's swelter had.

Marley's clothes had grown somewhat out of fashion in the years since his death—his pigtail, waistcoat, tights, and boots looked more like a stage costume than a proper businessman's attire. His chain of cashboxes, keys, padlocks, ledgers, deeds, and heavy purses wrought in steel was clasped about his middle. Scrooge thought its length must have diminished over the years, thanks to his friend's good works, but it was still a heavy burden, and Marley seemed glad of the opportunity, however fleeting, to rest.

On his otherwise barren chimneypiece, Scrooge kept a decanter of brandy and a pair of snifters (a long-ago Christmas gift from his nephew) for just such occasions. Only when his late partner was fully settled in the chair opposite did Scrooge rise and pour one glass nearly full, then dribble a few drops into the other. The full glass he passed to Marley; the other he kept for himself—not drinking, but periodically breathing the rich vapours that circulated in its depths. Marley had politely taken his usual chair, a ragged and decrepit affair that would be no worse for the fresh brandy stains Scrooge would find there next morning—for it might truly be said of Marley that he could not hold his liquor.

It occurred to Scrooge that he might remark on this defect in his friend's character, for he was much in the habit of making merry, but Marley's fixed, glazed eyes and the hot vapours that swirled his ghostly hair told Scrooge there was more import to this visit than desire for a friend's society and wit. Marley was often wont to sit with Scrooge when the living member of this peculiar pair suffered a sleepless night due to an undigested bit of beef, a blot of mustard, a crumb of cheese, or a fragment of an underdone potato, but tonight Marley downed his brandy and, as the stain spread slowly across the cushion, raised his face to the ceiling and let out a cry of such lament that Scrooge, in spite of himself, felt chilled to his marrow.

"What troubles you, good friend?" asked Scrooge, in as calm a voice as he could (for though he was quite content to chat with Marley for hours, he never forgot that his friend was a ghost, and he knew that mystery and terror might lurk around any corner of the conversation).

"I'm sorry to frighten you," said the ghost, not for a moment fooled by Scrooge's false composure, "but I begin to despair of ever breaking these chains." At this Marley rose and rattled the chains so that the sound echoed throughout the house, down the stairwell, across the yard below, and down the street, where gaslights flickered and neighbours abed shuddered in their sleep.

Scrooge waited until the echoes had died in the heavy evening air and the spectre had fallen back into his brandy-soaked chair. "You are not so fettered as when you first came to these rooms," he said. "Surely all your works in the past score of years have shortened the chains you bear. Surely you must be close on to earning your rest."

"These chains!" cried Marley, holding his arms aloft so that the chains dragged across the floor with a dull growl. "Since the night I enlisted the help of three spirits to turn you from a man of impervious selfishness to one who embraces all his fellow men with Christian love, I have been relieved of but five links."

"Five links!" said Scrooge, jumping to his feet and striding to the window, where the thick summer air slid into the room. "Five links! But you have laboured these twenty years to help me be a better man, to keep me on the track you so wisely set me upon that Christmas Eve that seems another life ago. How can all those years of devotion have lessened your burden only five links?" And this Scrooge shouted into the night, as if those who imprisoned his friend might be lurking outside his window and find themselves moved by his passionate testimony.

"Five links," said Marley dully, not moving from his chair. "It is the paradox of my curse that in order to shorten my chains I must do good for those who still live, yet I have forever lost the power to interfere in human affairs. Few of my fellow spectres have lost as many links as five, and most despair of ever lightening their loads."

Marley tilted his head back once again and opened his ghostly mouth, and more to stanch the wail that would curdle his blood than because he knew of any way to free Marley from his torment, Scrooge said, "What if there were a way?"

Marley froze, his mouth so wide that his face appeared nearly overwhelmed by its cavernous blackness. Then, slowly, silently, he lowered his gaze to the empty fireplace, pressed his thin lips together, and sat for several minutes, not wailing or howling or rattling his chains—sat for so long, in fact, that Scrooge began to wonder if ghosts could fall asleep. He was going over in his mind all of Marley's previous visits, trying to recall if such a thing had ever occurred, when the ghost parted his lips just enough to murmur, in a tone so low as to be nearly inaudible, "A way?"

Scrooge turned from the window to find Marley's gaze locked on him, and he almost thought he detected a spark of hope in the spirit's empty, passionless eyes. "Let us consider the problem as a business proposition," said Scrooge, encouraged by the bemused expression that seemed to wash over Marley's face. "You arranged for one man—that is, myself—to see the error of his ways and to waken his latent power for good on a single day, Christmas Day. For that your load was lightened by five links."

"True," said Marley, still not moving.

"One man, one day, five links," said Scrooge, who, now that he had begun to think in terms of numbers, was in familiar territory. He could see the solution to Marley's torment like a row of figures in a ledger laid out before him—a simple matter of arithmetic. "What if I told you," he said, "that I knew of a way to help hundreds, maybe thousands of people, and not just on one day, but on every day of the year? If one times one equals five links, three hundred and sixty-five times a thousand would free you of your chains a hundredfold."

"You were never as skilled with numbers as I, Ebenezer," said Marley. "I have changed you for more than a single day and you have been of aid to many others."

"But nonetheless," said Scrooge, "that goodwill is but a fraction of what I now envision."

"But you know it is not within my power to help the living," said Marley with a sigh, and he sank back into his chair and dropped his head onto his ghostly chest so that the two seemed almost to merge.

"Not possible for you, perhaps," said Scrooge, now trembling with the excitement of the vision unfolding before him, "but what if it were possible for me? What if I could help a thousand people or a hundred thousand, but I couldn't do it without you? Wouldn't that count for something?"

Without realising how it happened, for he never saw Marley budge from his chair, Scrooge found himself enveloped in a cold so chilling he could not move. It was a feeling that would have struck terror in the hearts of most men, but Scrooge knew it to be Marley's embrace. Cold though it was, he could feel the joy in his friend's spirit and the hope in his dormant, ghostly heart. And for the first time in all the years he had known Marley, thirty-two years in life and twenty years in death, he felt something else. A single icy tear dropped from Marley's eye onto Scrooge's cheek.

A moment later, Marley stepped back and looked his friend in the eyes. "What do you need from me?" he asked.

"First," said Scrooge, without the slightest hesitation, "I shall require three spirits."

❧

The First of the Three Spirits

Many a person in Scrooge's excited state (and I daresay you are one of them) would have shunned sleep, know-ing as he did that his night would be haunted by not one but three spectres beyond that which had already paid him a visit. Not so for Scrooge, though. He climbed into bed, pulled the curtains shut around him, and was soon as sound asleep as you or I would be on a cold winter's night when a fire burned in the grate, the covers were piled high atop us, and we had nothing more to worry our minds than to wonder if the snow would stop falling by daybreak.

Scrooge awoke in blackness so complete that he knew it must be near the hour of the first ghost's coming—for only at such an hour, deep in the night, would total darkness reign in midsummer. The air sat stiller than still around him and no sounds drifted up from the street to his open window. He was endeavouring to pierce the gloom with his sparkling eyes (which somehow continued to glitter despite the dearth of light) when the chimes of a neighbouring church struck the four quarters. Holding his breath with excitement, he listened for the hour. One. No more. The hour had come!

Before Scrooge could leap from his bed to greet the visitor he knew must even then be arriving in his rooms, the curtains of his bed, at his feet, were drawn aside by a hand. In an instant Scrooge was sitting at the foot of the bed, his warm feet dangling above the floor, his face inches from the smooth and youthful visage of his unearthly visitor. How well he remembered that supernatural figure that hovered before him—though they had met only once, a score of years ago. The flowing hair of ancient white so incongruous with the tender bloom of rose on the unsullied cheeks, the muscular arms and legs bare to the warm air, the tunic of purest white, the sprig of holly, and above all the clear winter light that sprung from his head. Scrooge felt as if he were meeting an old friend, and he could not have been more delighted if the dearest companion of his youth had materialised in his rooms.

"Welcome, gentle Spirit!" cried Scrooge. "I thank you for coming to my aid on a night when you should, by all rights, be at rest."

The Ghost of Christmas Past—for that, of course, is who stood before Mr. Scrooge—tossed back his head, shook his white locks, and let forth a long, musical sigh. "It is indeed many a year since I have ventured abroad in this sultry season, but I carry my winter with me." Scrooge observed that the spirit's sigh had frosted the windows and raised gooseflesh on his own arms. "What business brings me here?"

"The welfare of my dear friend Jacob Marley, and of a thousand others who suffer in this city tonight."

The ghost held out his hand. "I once guided you on a journey," he said, "but now you have summoned me and shall be my guide. Whither would you?"

Scrooge laid his hand on that of the ghost and clasped him gently. "Before we journey to that past which is your domain, we must collect another passenger," he said. But before he had uttered the name of that soul, who lay asleep and unsuspecting a few miles away, he and the ghost had passed through the wall. Scrooge was afforded no more than a glimpse of the lights of London before he found himself standing, with his spectral companion, at the foot of a bed not unlike his own, though the room in which it stood was cluttered with papers that seemed to cascade from every surface (of which there were many). Wildeyed and afraid for his life, his hair jutting out from his head at unlikely angles, sat Scrooge's nephew, bolt upright and clinging to the bedsheet, which he had pulled nearly over his head in fright.

"Merry Christmas, nephew!" bellowed Scrooge.

"U-u-u-uncle?" stuttered the disbelieving nephew.

"I'd like you to meet my nephew, Freddie," said Scrooge, as casually as if he were introducing two acquaintances on a street corner. "Freddie, this is a dear friend of mine who once helped save my life and tonight will help save yours. May I present the Ghost of Christmas Past."

If possible, Freddie's eyes opened even wider. From sheer force of habit, he managed to whisper, "Very pleased to make your acquaintance, Mr. . . ."

"You may call me Spirit," said the ghost jovially.

"And what is your business here, Spirit?" asked Freddie, with a bureaucratic air that belied his continued unease.

"As I said, nephew, we come for your welfare."

The nephew, now fully awake and of the belief that he might dispose of these unwelcome visitors in the same manner that he disposed of those members of the public who deigned to wander into his office in Whitehall, noted that a night of unbroken rest would have been more conducive to that end.

"Take heed!" cried the Spirit, rattling all authority out of poor Freddie, who now, if he had been wearing boots, would have been shaking in them.

"Rise and walk with us," said Scrooge. "You must see the past ere we plot your future." With this he laid one hand on his nephew and the other on the Spirit, and in a twinkling (though Freddie might have been more likely to describe it as a trembling) the trio found themselves in a cold stone room. The air was dank and stale, the only light a pale and hazy aura that seeped through an iron-barred window high overhead. The room was unfurnished (it was, in fact, so small it would have admitted little more than a single kitchen stool) and Freddie at first thought it empty. A low groan from behind him he took to be the voice of the ghost, until that spectre removed his cap and the room was flooded with the white light that flowed from his pate.

Freddie turned on his feet to take in the entire room, which he now saw to be no more than six feet square. When he saw the source of the groan he stopped in horror, his breath catching in his throat. Against his better judgment, he stared transfixed at the figure before him. The woman lay slumped against the rough stone wall, her hands and feet fastened to those same stones with chains as heavy as those that encumbered the ghost of Jacob Marley—a spirit which Freddie, prior to that night, had dismissed as his uncle's fancy. The woman's clothes were so ragged as to be nearly superfluous and her hair was matted far worse than the fur of the stray dogs on London's streets.

"What godforsaken prison is this?" choked Freddie.

"Not a prison," said the ghost, to whom Freddie now paid rapt attention. "An asylum. St. Luke's Hospital for Lunatics. This creature came here in hopes of a cure for her madness."

"This cannot be," gasped Freddie. "Such inhumanity is surely a thing of the past."

"So it is," said the ghost. "Perhaps you forget who I am. But this is a past you must see."

"She was a governess," said Scrooge, "working for a respectable family for seven years before she became ill. Now she has been chained to that wall for as many years, with no hope of salvation."

The woman groaned again, a quiet and resigned sort of groan that seeped out of her like the last of the air out of a squeeze-box. She took no notice of either her visitors or the light they brought to her cell. Freddie reached out to touch her filthy shoulder but felt nothing but cold air.

"She is but the shadow of what has been," said the ghost. "She has no consciousness of us."

"What day is this?" asked Freddie, his eyes still on the wretched creature at his feet.

"Christmas Day," answered the ghost. "A Christmas before you were brought into this world, though not before your uncle heard the first chorus of 'Merry Christmas' strike his ears."

"But how can doctors treat a poor woman like this?" asked Freddie.

"Coercion for the outward man, and rabid physicking for the inward man, were then the specifics for lunacy," replied the ghost. "Chains, straw, filthy solitude, darkness, and starvation; spinning in whirligigs, corporal punishment, gagging, continued intoxication; nothing was too wildly extravagant, nothing too monstrously cruel to be prescribed by mad-doctors."

"And what is to happen to this soul?" asked Freddie, tears gathering in his eyes as he felt unfamiliar emotions coursing through him.

But the ghost only replied, "Remember this Christmas and what you saw here."

At this Freddie finally tore his eyes away from the woman and turned on his uncle. "Why did you bring me here, Uncle Ebenezer?" he cried, tears of despair and anger now streaming down his face. "Why do you show me this sight and tell me there is nothing I can do?"

"There is much you can do," replied Scrooge calmly, exchanging a knowing smile with the ghost. "But it is time we moved on."

As the room dissolved around them, and the figure of the poor woman faded into the shadow that it was, and then into nothingness, Freddie heard an upwelling of cries, as if a thousand other inmates of that ghastly place let out their miseries at once. As the sound seemed just about to overwhelm them, it suddenly stopped, and Freddie found himself standing in a narrow street that curved downhill to the river, with some stairs at the end, where pedestrians might become passengers of the craft that plied the waters of the Thames. At the top of those stairs, where Freddie and his companions now found themselves, was a crazy old house with a wharf of its own, which must have abutted on the water when the tide was in, but now abutted only mud. The sun hung low in the sky and there was a winter chill in the air.

"I know this place," said Scrooge excitedly, pointing to the sign that hung upon the waterside warehouse. MURDSTONE AND GRINBY'S, it proclaimed. Though Freddie was still adjusting to the fact that it was no longer either nighttime or summer and that he was no longer in either St. Luke's or his own lodgings, Scrooge grinned with delight at his realisation: Not only did the grim and grimy warehouse inhabit the end of a street in Blackfriars; it also inhabited the pages of the novel that currently rested atop Scrooge's bedside table a few miles and some decades hence.

The travellers ventured inside the warehouse, inured as they were to the horrors of what they would see by the fact that they visited only shadows of what had been. Within they discovered panelled rooms, discoloured with the dirt and smoke of a hundred years. The floors and staircases were decaying and from the cellars they could hear the squeaking and scuffling of old grey rats. The dirt and rottenness of the place was worse than Freddie had imagined even from its dour exterior.

A large room on the ground floor of the warehouse rang with stern voices, clanking of machinery, splashing of water, and a score of other noises, making conversation amongst the visitors impossible, but the Spirit led Scrooge and Freddie to a dim and quieter corner, where an especially noxious odour hung in the air. Bent over a small table was a gaunt boy who could not have been more than twelve. His face was drawn and without expression, and his vacant eyes seemed to focus on something far beyond the work of his hands. His clothes were worn and ragged and his face and hands so dirty as to make his racial origins a matter of some uncertainty. The acrid smell in his corner of the warehouse rose from a pot of glue, into which he repeatedly dipped a brush. With this smoking concoction inches from his nose, he brushed the back of a paper label, which he then transferred to an empty bottle. This process he repeated some dozens of times in the few moments that Scrooge and Freddie observed him. His hands were cracked and burned from the glue and his eyes red from the fumes. As he placed each freshly labelled bottle to the side he let out a rattling cough.

"His father is in debtors' prison at the Marshalsea," said the Spirit. "Strange that if a man has twenty pounds a year for his income, and spends nineteen pounds nineteen shillings and sixpence, he is happy, but if he spends twenty pounds one he is miserable, as are his children."

"A talented boy he was," added Scrooge. "Such promise."

Without pausing to ask how Scrooge knew the young lad, Freddie asked, "How long must he work like this?"

"Sixteen hours a day," replied the Spirit, "with a half hour for tea." Though Freddie had meant to ask for how many days or weeks or, God forbid, months longer the boy would be employed in this dreadful work, he reeled at the thought that for even a single day a child should be forced to work such hours in such conditions.

"And today is . . ." said Freddie.

"Today is Christmas Day," said the Spirit.

"But something must be done!" cried Freddie, anger boiling inside him. "Surely such a child should be in school. And no one should work like this on Christmas Day. Are there no laws, no regulations?"

"Surely," said the Spirit, "there *are* such laws. But I am

the Ghost of Christmas Past, and the rules that provide Greek and Latin for a child instead of endless hours of drudgery are quite recent." It could be argued that Greek and Latin were another form of drudgery, Scrooge reflected, but he couldn't deny they were a substantially more humane form.

"It's a travesty," said Freddie. "If I had been alive to see such things, I should have marched straight to Parliament and not rested until something was done."

"Would you?" asked Scrooge, smiling, for he could almost hear the chains falling from Marley.

"Wait a moment," said Freddie, paying no heed to his uncle but rounding on the ghost, his anger welling up red in his face. "That woman you showed me at the asylum—should not the Lunacy Commission have done something for her? We should file a report. Such abuses are not allowed to . . ." His voice trailed off as the ghost drifted before him through the wall of the factory. In the next moment, the three figures hovered over the murky waters of the Thames.

"I suppose at the time there was no Lunacy Commission," mumbled Freddie, oblivious to his seemingly precarious position in midair.

"Not then," said the ghost. "But problems can be addressed. Shall we pay her another visit?" In an instant the three figures found themselves again within the walls of the asylum.

"Is it still Christmas past?" asked Freddie, his voice echo-ing in the stony silence.

"Quite recent past," said the ghost. "A mere five Christ-mases ago."

They stood in a long, low gallery with a few windows on one side and a great many doors leading to sleeping cells on the other. Several women were seated on benches around a caged fireplace, all silent, except one. Though there was noth-ing in her hands, she sewed a mad sort of seam and scolded some imaginary person. Except the scolding woman, every patient in the room either silently looked at the fire or silently looked at the ground—or rather through the ground, and at heaven knows what beyond. Freddie sensed no happiness, but neither did he sense the unjustified misery of the woman he had seen on his previous visit.

It was a relief to come to a workroom, with coloured prints over the mantel shelf and china shepherdesses upon it, fur-nished also with tables, a carpet, stuffed chairs, and an open fire. There was a great difference between the demeanour of the occupants of this apartment and that of the inmates of the other room. They were neither so listless nor so sad. Although they did not speak much, they worked with earnestness and diligence, most at some sort of needlework. After a few moments, Scrooge hurried off in the direction of music, which had begun playing in the distance. Freddie followed close on his heels, with the ghost drifting languidly behind.

In another gallery a ball had begun. Freddie hunted for the figure of the young woman. Amongst the dancers, there were the patients usually to be found in all such asylums. There was the brisk, vain, pippin-faced little old lady, in a fantastic cap, proud of her foot and ankle; there was the old-young woman, with dishevelled long light hair, spare figure, and weird gentility; there was the vacantly laughing girl, requiring now and then a warning finger to admonish her; there was the quiet young woman, almost well, and soon going out. The dancers were not all patients. Amongst them, and dancing with right goodwill, were attendants, male and female— pleasant-looking men, not at all realising the conventional idea of "keepers," and pretty women, gracefully though not at all inappropriately dressed, and with looks and smiles as sparkling as one might hope to see in any dance in any place.

The moment the dance was over, away the porter ran, not in the least out of breath, to help light up the tree. Presently it stood in the centre of its room, growing out of the floor, a blaze of light and glitter, blossoming in that place for the first time in a hundred years. Shining beside it, shining above them all, and shining everywhere, the resident officer's wife. Freddie could tell in an instant, as she helped the inmates to pass round the tree and admire, that heaven had inspired her clear head and strong heart to have no Christmas wish beyond this place, but to look upon it as her home, and on its inmates as her afflicted children.

"I think you'll agree, there's been an improvement," said the ghost.

"One only needed to pass some proper laws," said Freddie indignantly, as if this were the simplest thing in the world.

"Yes," said Scrooge, "such things can do good at times."

"But where is the young woman?" asked Freddie. "You promised I should see what became of her."

"Not a young woman," said the ghost quietly. "Youth slips away rapidly in such a place under the best of circumstances, and it is two score years since our last visit." The ghost nodded towards the tree, where the sparkling face of the resident officer's wife was greeting the last of the inmates. It was the scolding woman who had been sewing a purposeless seam. She still scolded her unseen companion, and looked through the tree as if it were not there, but the hostess nonetheless ushered her round the tree, pointing out its delights. When the pair reemerged from behind the tree, Freddie saw a hint of contentment in the eyes of the old woman.

"One might not say that she was saved," said the ghost,

Even a very old friend of mine might benefit from a liberal voice in the Commons," said Scrooge, thinking of Marley's burden.

"But, uncle," cried Freddie, again thinking of practicalities, "how am I to be elected to Parliament? I am nothing but a clerk in Whitehall."

"Have you not heard?" replied his uncle. "England is a democracy now. Even a clerk in Whitehall may become a member of Parliament. I daresay the day is not far off when a novelist may become prime minister. But as for you, my boy—let your resolve be sufficient for now. We shall discuss the details of your career as a social reformer by the light of day. Now, you'd best be off to bed before my next visitor arrives." With that Scrooge picked up a book from his nephew's table and, settling deeper in the chair, began to read, paying Freddie no more mind. Freddie turned to discover the door to his bedroom open once more, and he shortly enjoyed a deep sleep and dreams in which powdered wigs, impassioned debates, committees, commissions, and ministers swirled around him in a dance more curious still than that which he had witnessed at the asylum. Entranced by such visions, he rested well.

※

The Second of the Three Spirits

I t so happened that on that same evening, whilst Scrooge entertained his departed partner in his gloomy rooms, Mr. Pleasant sat with Mr. Portly in their drawing room in Mayfair, attended by a butler known to them only as Johnson, who had kept their brandy replenished for some hours. They had discussed, as was their wont, first the relative fortunes of various corporations; second, the general economic outlook; third, as the brandy began to do its work, the personal habits of certain bank employees; and finally, just before falling asleep in their chairs to the amusement of Johnson, who retired to a comfortable bed, their speculations about the personal habits of certain bank customers. Johnson assumed that, as usual, he needn't disturb them until breakfast.

Scrooge awoke in the middle of a prodigiously raucous

snore, for his nephew possessed no novels, not even those written by the sort of novelist who might one day become prime minister, and, forced to read a book on international trade regulations, he had quickly fallen into a deep slumber. He was restored to consciousness in the nick of time and for the especial purpose of holding a conference with the second messenger dispatched to him by Jacob Marley.

The room in which he awoke was the same as that in which he had dozed off, but it had undergone what you and I would consider a surprising transformation, though to Scrooge it was completely expected. The walls and ceiling were so hung with living green that the chamber looked a perfect grove, from every part of which bright, gleaming berries glistened. The crisp leaves of holly, mistletoe, and ivy reflected back the light, as if so many little mirrors had been scattered there. Heaped up on the floor, to form a kind of throne, were turkeys, geese, game, poultry, great joints of meat, suckling pigs, long wreaths of sausages, mince pies, plum puddings, barrels of oysters, red-hot chestnuts, cherry-cheeked apples, juicy oranges, luscious pears, immense twelfth-cakes, and seething bowls of punch that made the chamber dim with their delicious steam. Scrooge marvelled that his nephew could sleep soundly in the next room whilst such an aroma of sweetness filled the air.

Sitting amongst it all, or rather reclining, for he was nearly supine, rested a jolly giant, glorious to see, and as familiar to Scrooge as was the innkeeper who prepared his nightly feast. There was the simple green robe, or mantle, bordered with white fur. There were the bare feet and chest. There was the wreath of holly on the head, and there, amongst its leaves, the shining icicles that defied the summer weather. Scrooge's face sparkled with delight to see a figure so alike in counte-nance and raiment to his former companion.

"Welcome, good friend," he said, skipping round the Spirit with as much glee as his old knees would allow. The Spirit followed Scrooge's capering with twinkling eyes and a genial face, and answered him in a cheery voice that rent the air with joy.

"My dear Scrooge," he said. "How well you have come to know my brothers these past twenty years."

"Indeed," replied Scrooge, "I count them amongst my best of friends. I believe, at times, that they alone understand my peculiar habits and attitudes."

"You are as one of our family," said the phantom, gently laying a hand on Scrooge's head, at which the old man blushed so deeply the glow might have lit the room, were a fire not burning merrily in the grate. "But our time is short, and you have set us a difficult task. Shall we begin?"

Scrooge reached out a wrinkled hand and grasped the hem

of the Spirit's robe, and holly, mistletoe, red berries, ivy, turkeys, geese, game, poultry, meat, pigs, sausages, oysters, pies, puddings, fruit, and punch all vanished instantly. In their place was a dim parlour, the lamps doused and the grate empty, the only light filtering in through the open window from the streetlight below. In two round stuffed chairs slumped two round stuffed gentlemen, snoring in unison, empty brandy glasses at their elbows. In an instant a fire leapt in the grate and the chairs leant forward, tumbling their occupants onto the hearthrug, where they sat rubbing their eyes, wondering if breakfast had come already and why Johnson had lit a fire on such a hot day.

"Merry Christmas, friends!" shouted Scrooge, adding further confusion to the faces of Messrs. Pleasant and Portly until the latter, realising that only one person in London would make such an exclamation on the shortest night of the year, stumbled to his feet and responded with a scowl.

"Ebenezer Scrooge! Bah!"

To which his companion added, "Humbug!"

"We've not much time and much to do," said Scrooge, ignoring the displeasure of the freshly disturbed gentlemen. "Perhaps I should first introduce you."

And here the eyes of Messrs. Portly and Pleasant widened in a way that was usually reserved for surprisingly large deposits received at the bank, for they observed, lounging on a mountain of turkeys, geese, plum puddings, and holly, the spirit who had borne Scrooge to their parlour. The Spirit remained silent, but his eyes glittered and he smiled broadly at the two dumbstruck gentlemen as he gobbled an especially large pudding.

"He . . . he . . . he looks like a child," stammered Mr. Portly as the Spirit wiped his mouth on his voluminous sleeve.

"Indeed, you are exactly correct!" squealed Scrooge with delight.

"I am the Ghost of Christmas Present," said the Spirit, trying ineffectually to suppress a giggle. "I shall not be of age for another six months." With this he ripped the leg off a turkey and began to gnaw on the juicy meat.

"'Tis no matter," said Scrooge. "Young or old, he will take us where we need to go this night."

"Where I need to go," said Mr. Pleasant in a tone that belied his epithet, "is to bed. I suggest the rest of you do the same." He marched towards the door, only to find his path barricaded by an enormous fold of fur as the Spirit tossed the hem of his mantle in front of the fleeing financier.

"If . . . if you will forgive us, Mr. Scrooge," said Mr. Portly in a shaky voice, "we really must be abed; our business begins quite early tomorrow."

"It is tomorrow," laughed Scrooge, pointing to the clock on the chimneypiece, which was about to strike the quarter after two. "And your business begins now." With the final syllable of this proclamation, Scrooge's voice acquired an intensity that Messrs. Pleasant and Portly found more menacing than the giant, who now flicked a bare turkey bone into the fire.

"Shall we go?" asked the Spirit, standing and shaking the crumbs out of his mantle. It was a remarkable quality of the ghost (which Scrooge had observed in his brother) that, notwithstanding his gigantic size, he could accommodate himself to any place with ease. For the residents of that house, the sight of this colossal figure standing comfortably in their parlour finally shocked them into the realisation that they would not be slipping quietly off to their bedchambers, but that some ominous adventure lay waiting for them. In another moment, the Spirit had grabbed the unsuspecting gentlemen by the hands; the parlour, the fire, and the trappings of Christmas had all disappeared; and the quartet stood in the cold winter air of a black, dilapidated lane flanked by tenements that looked as though they might topple forward into the street at any moment.

"Welcome, gentlemen, welcome," said Scrooge. "I daresay you have seldom ventured into this part of London. Not so many customers here as in Mayfair, no doubt."

"Is this about those charity cheques, Mr. Scrooge?" enquired Mr. Pleasant. "Surely you must know that you could write a thousand cheques for fifty pounds and the London poor would still be with us."

"Indeed," said Mr. Portly, shaking his head, "one person simply cannot change the plight of the unfortunate."

"But one person might change the plight of one unfortunate," said Scrooge. "One person may even change the plight of ten, or a score, or a hundred unfortunates. Let us go in, shall we?"

On entering the nearest house, the men were met with a fetid smell that made further ingress difficult. Nevertheless, clutching their sleeves across their noses, they pressed on, down a dark and filthy staircase. As parasites appear on the ruined human wretch, so this ruined shelter had bred a crowd of foul vermin that crawled in and out of gaps in walls and boards, fetching and carrying fever and sowing evil in their every footprint.

They emerged amongst a range of damp and gloomy stone vaults beneath the ground. The filth of humanity oozed up around their feet. From ahead in the near darkness, they heard a soft moan.

"You don't really mean to say that human beings live down in these wretched dungeons?" asked Mr. Pleasant.

"Live down here and die down here, too, very often," replied Scrooge solemnly, pushing open a door to reveal a small chamber. The room was colder than the street outside. No fire could be placed in the grate, for there was no grate, the stone vault having been intended originally for keeping a small quantity of coal to supply lodgers in a room above. Seated against the wall on the wet floor were four wretched beings, who seemed human only in form. As Scrooge informed his companions, they had once occupied rooms on an upper floor of the same house. The father, whose head lolled loosely on his shoulders, had been a weaver, and had supported his family passably well until a dry spell of work forced him to burn his loom to keep the children warm. The bedsteads, chairs, and tables he had already burned. Now, as his whisperings revealed, he only prayed that death might take his children quickly, and with little pain.

"But what can we do?" asked Mr. Portly. "There are so many living in such conditions."

"There are not so many here," said Scrooge. "There are only four. Here is a man who needs only enough money to buy a loom and he might ransom his family from this prison."

"Surely there are relief societies to help just such a person," said Mr. Pleasant, averting his gaze from the hollow eyes of the mother, who cradled her children in her lap.

"Why, certainly," said Scrooge cheerfully. "The Society for the Relief of Distress undertakes just such endeavours."

"Well, we had best contact them," said Mr. Portly.

"They are a bit shy of funding at the moment," said Scrooge. "It seems the bank refused payment on a fifty-pound donation just this morning. A mere fraction of that would have saved this family."

"You don't mean to say," said Mr. Pleasant, "that they will . . ."

"I am but the ghost of this year's Christmas," said the Spirit, breaking his silence. "I cannot tell what is to pass on Christmases yet to come. Yet I would be surprised if any of my younger brothers ever meet these souls."

Mr. Pleasant opened his mouth as if to remark on this prediction, but before he could speak, the Spirit had once again taken hold of his hand, and that of his companion, and the dungeon fell away beneath them. They found themselves standing in a narrow paved yard hemmed in by high walls duly spiked at the top. From this yard they passed into a small cell, which, though its occupant was a prisoner, was luxurious in comparison to the home they had just left behind. In one corner stood a simple wooden bedstead and next to it a stool and a writing desk, on which lay a few sheets of paper. From a small window high in one wall a hint of daylight filtered into the room. Seated on the stool was a man in ragged clothes with dishevelled hair, scratching away with a quill.

"I know this man!" cried Mr. Portly. "Or I know what he was, for the last time I saw him his hair was kempt, his cravat exquisite, and the sheen fresh on his breeches."

"Why, of course," said Mr. Pleasant. "He was a customer of the bank. That is, he . . . he . . ." And Mr. Pleasant stuttered into silence as he dragged the depths of his mind for the details of the prisoner's long-forgotten business with the bank.

"He was a debtor," said Mr. Portly slowly. "He owed ten shillings and sixpence and came to the bank for a loan of the sum."

"Indeed," said Mr. Pleasant, the memory swimming to the surface from the murky past. "We could do nothing to help him, of course, but such a small debt must have easily been repaid."

"Must it?" asked the Spirit, with a wink at Scrooge.

"His debt was repaid, to be sure," said Scrooge. "And the ten and six he borrowed from a moneylender has compounded, as of today, into three hundred and sixteen pounds, eight shillings, and twopence."

"Oh, he shall never be able to pay such a debt," said Mr. Pleasant, who now had a clear picture of the man's past financial irresponsibility before him.

"Indeed, it seems unlikely," said Mr. Portly, peering over

the man's shoulder. "He seems to do nothing but write letters to acquaintances asking for assistance. He's not likely to keep pace with the interest in that manner."

"Some useful occupation is what he should pursue," said Mr. Pleasant.

"And what useful occupation would you have him pursue here in debtors' prison?" asked Scrooge, his voice tinged with impatience. "What useful occupation could he possibly pursue when his interest is compounded at a rate that would make you and Mr. Portly paupers in six months' time? And to think what a small sum would have saved him once."

"Would have saved him?" said Mr. Portly quietly. "Do you mean to say there is no hope whatsoever?"

"That is not for me to say," said the Spirit.

"He was a kind man, as I recall," said Mr. Pleasant. "A right jolly fellow."

"Ten and six," muttered Scrooge. "'Tis a shame to throw away a life for such a small sum."

"I wonder if perhaps—" Mr. Portly began, but his rumi-nation was interrupted by the Spirit, who, without speaking, grabbed each banker by the hand and whisked them away, or so it seemed, on the very air, until the broken man, the locked cell, and the whole of the debtors' prison melted away below them in the mist which now swirled across the city.

Then the strange quartet—Messrs. Pleasant and Portly still dressed for dinner, though their ties were loosened, Scrooge in his nightclothes, and the towering Spirit in his glowing green mantle—seemed to drop gently from the sky and settled in a tiny court where they were nearly overcome by the reek of malodourous fumes rising from an accumulation of sewage and refuse that lay heaped in every corner and under every foot.

"I doubt you've visited any of the rookeries of our city," remarked Scrooge as if he were showing off a row of fine houses on Park Lane. "Welcome."

What surrounded them left Messrs. Pleasant and Portly speechless for some time, as Scrooge led the way through the dark neighbourhood: wretched houses with broken windows patched with rags and paper; every room let out to a different family, and in many instances to two or even three—fruit and "sweetstuff" manufacturers in the cellars, barbers and red herring vendors in the front parlours, cobblers in the back, a bird fancier on the first floor, three families on the second, starvation in the attics, Irishmen in the passage, a "musician" in the front kitchen, a charwoman and five hungry children in the back one; filth everywhere—a gutter before the houses and a drain behind—clothes drying, and slops emptying from the windows; girls of fourteen or fifteen with matted hair, walking about barefoot and in white greatcoats, almost their only covering; boys of all ages, in coats of all sizes and no coats at all; men and women, in every variety of scanty and dirty apparel, lounging, scolding, drinking, smoking, squabbling, fighting, and swearing.

Scrooge led the strange, unseen party through one of the houses. The rooms were seldom more than eight feet square, the furnishings often consisting of nothing more than the pickings from nearby rubbish heaps. The grime on the walls was so thick it streamed to the floor. In one room, they discovered a mother and six children—the children shortly to be banished to the streets for several hours whilst their mother used the room to earn the money to feed them in the only way she could. Room after room, house after house, court after court, Scrooge led the two bankers until they had all but forgotten their supernatural companion and could think of nothing but filth, squalor, disease, and death—for it was death, more than anything else, that infused these pestilential streets.

Finally, they could bear it no more. "Do not torture us this way, Ebenezer!" cried Mr. Portly. "There is only so much misery a man can take."

Scrooge pointed to a man who lay against the crumbling wall of a nearby house. "Would you say that he has reached that limit?"

"Surely," said Mr. Pleasant, "we might find a way to help some of these souls."

"So I thought," said Scrooge. "That is why I wrote a cheque for fifty pounds to the Metropolitan Sanitary Association. They had hoped to pull these tumbling, disease-ridden houses down, to clean the streets and courts, to replace the current buildings with new and clean homes for those unfortunate enough not to be born into banking families."

At that moment, Mr. Portly became suddenly aware again of the presence of the Spirit, who now lurked in a shadowy corner of the court in which they stood. It was not the glistening of the icicles encircling the Spirit's head that drew his attention, nor the thought that the feast with which the ghost had first surrounded himself might do much good in these quarters; rather, it was something protruding from the skirts of the Spirit, something with all the appearance of a clawlike foot, as shrivelled as that of the dying children they had witnessed in the surrounding houses.

"Is there a child beneath your robes, Spirit?" asked Mr. Portly. "Or do the shadows merely bring some bit of rubbish to life before my tired eyes?"

"It might be rubbish, for the flesh there is upon it," was the Spirit's sorrowful reply. "Look here."

From the folds of its robe, the ghost brought two children, wretched, abject, frightful, hideous, miserable—a reflection of all the bankers had seen on their recent tour. They were a boy and a girl. Yellow, meagre, ragged, scowling, wolfish; but prostrate, too, in their humility. Where graceful youth should have filled their features out and touched them with its freshest tints, a stale and shrivelled hand, like that of age, had pinched and twisted them, and pulled them into shreds.

"Whence came these children?" asked Mr. Portly. "Spirit, did you find them in some room of this rookery, or are . . . are they yours?"

"They are Man's," said the Spirit, looking down upon them. "This boy is Ignorance. This girl is Want. Beware them both, and all of their degree, but most of all beware this boy, for on his brow I see that written which is Doom, unless the writing be erased. You may be ignorant no more, but you must banish the ignorance of others."

"Have these poor children no refuge or resource?" cried Mr. Pleasant. "Can no one show them an ounce of liberality?"

"Liberality is not the business of a bank," said the Spirit, turning on him with his own words. And as the banker opened his mouth to reply . . .

The bell struck three.

The three men now found themselves back where their tour had begun, that being the drawing room in the house of Messrs. Pleasant and Portly. The two residents of that place once again sat in their chairs by the fireplace and a lamp burned on the table between them. Opposite, on a cushioned divan, sat Scrooge.

"I have been thinking," said Mr. Pleasant, as if the conversation was a mere continuation of their earlier discussion and no supernatural beings had disturbed their evening. "The bank has other customers besides Mr. Scrooge."

"My thoughts exactly," said Mr. Portly. "Customers who might be more . . . shall we say more economically suited to the sort of largesse for which Mr. Scrooge makes so compelling a case."

The two bankers took no notice of Scrooge, and the old man almost wondered if he had become a ghost himself at some point during his nocturnal travels. If so, he thought, he hoped the afterlife would provide more stimulating adventures than eavesdropping on the conversations of financiers. He slid down low in the divan, rested his head against a cushion, and felt himself drifting away to the soothing tones of Messrs. Pleasant and Portly's excited chatter.

"If we were to approach a few clients . . ."

"A few selected clients . . ."

"A few specially selected clients . . ."

"Clients of means . . ."

"Clients of substantial means . . ."

"I know just the lady. . . ."

"I know just the gentleman. . . ."

❧

The Last of the Three Spirits

When Scrooge awoke, he beheld neither the sleeping forms of Messrs. Pleasant and Portly nor the familiar surroundings of his own room, but only, drifting towards him through the stagnant air of a dimly lit street, a frighteningly familiar figure. When he had struck his bargain with Jacob Marley what seemed like days ago, Scrooge had known this moment would come, but he had tried, in the intervening hours, to push all thought of the third and final spirit from his mind, for facing that ghost was a horror he was loath to repeat.

Scrooge lowered himself onto one knee and bent his head down so that he saw only the black hem of the cloak that enveloped the ghost. "Greetings, Spirit," he whispered. "Our time is short, and I know you to be a ghost of few words, so let us undertake with haste the task that brings you here."

To this speech the Spirit made no response, but merely floated above Scrooge and sniffed the night air from somewhere deep within its mantle, as if it had not smelled the air of the outdoors for many a month and even the dank fumes of a hot summer night were refreshment to it.

Though Scrooge had followed this Spirit many years ago, and suffered no permanent injury for its company, his legs still trembled as he climbed to his feet, and his breath came stuttering to his lips as he muttered, "Lead on, Spirit. I have travelled far and laboured hard this night, and I would rest yet before morning."

The Spirit raised a spectral hand from its cloak and pointed into the receding darkness of the street in which they stood. Taking this to mean that he should lead the way, Scrooge stepped past the ghost and felt a chill from the crown of his head to the tips of his toes. The heat of the night did little to comfort the old man, who wobbled down the street shivering, knowing full well the Spirit drifted just behind him.

Though he walked at a pace that might be expected from a man of his age passing through the streets in his nightclothes, the city seemed to fold in upon Scrooge with increasing rapidity, and it was no more than five minutes later that he found himself in a dark street of Camden Town, as shabby, dingy, damp, and mean a neighbourhood as one would desire to see.

Before him was a familiar door and in another moment he found himself, and the awful Spirit, inside the door, observing the scene before the grate.

In a chair by the hearth sat a man who might have been fifty or seventy, for all the dim light showed of his features. As it happened, Scrooge knew the man's age to the day, for he had marked Bob Cratchit's birthday annually for the past twenty years. Bob sat with his back to his visitors, reading the latest monthly installment of some popular novel. Scrooge was not timid about disturbing his partner's peace.

"How many times have I told you, Cratchit, to move from this four-room hovel to some abode in a cleaner quarter of the city?"

"Mr. Scrooge!" cried Cratchit, dropping his reading on the floor and jumping to his feet with a start. "I did not hear you come in. Is not the hour a bit late for you to be about in your nightclothes?"

Cratchit had, in fact, long suspected that Scrooge lived on the edge of sanity, and now it seemed that his partner had plunged into the abyss and would be making the journey to Bedlam at long last. But Scrooge was as sane as you or I and merely continued to reprimand his former clerk.

"And haven't I told you that there's no need to call me Mr. Scrooge, nor has there been any reason since you became my partner twenty years ago? I have a Christian name, and though it may not be a thing of beauty, I daresay if it was good enough for the vicar who doused me in holy water, it is good enough for Bob Cratchit."

"Ebenezer," said Cratchit, sliding sideways across the wall until he reached the poker and grasping that tool in case the need for a weapon arose, "I think it would be best if we took you home to get some sleep."

"But then you always were a creature of habit," said Scrooge, ignoring his partner's suggestion. "You never could call me anything but Mr. Scrooge, you never could live anywhere but here, and you never did much like taking days off to visit your family. Except Christmas Day, of course."

"Really, Mr. Scrooge," said Cratchit, "I think . . ." But what Cratchit thought was forever lost, for at that moment he saw the dark figure lurking by the doorway, its skeletal hand now reaching out towards him in a slow, beckoning motion.

"We need to take a journey," said Scrooge. "Come." Cratchit let the poker clatter to the floor and came.

Through the streets of Camden Town and back towards the city the unseen trio made their way in silence. Though Scrooge knew they were travelling towards Christmas yet to come, he could not, from the weather, have guessed the time of year, for the air felt both cold and hot. What vapours came from the Spirit and what from the weather, he knew not. The night and the city seemed endless, and Scrooge had begun to despair that the Spirit would fulfill his mission, when at last they slipped the bonds of darkness and stood in a brightly lit nursery, where a young woman was serving tea cakes to three small children. There was a Christmas tree in the corner, decorated with gleaming ornaments, and beneath it a wooden locomotive brightly painted in green and gold.

"What did Grandmother mean," said the youngest child, a little girl no more than four, "when she said she would take us to the seaside next summer?"

The eldest child looked, to Scrooge, to be a boy of about ten, and his two younger sisters looked to him with a gleam of admiration as he answered this question.

"That we shall have a glorious time together with her. You shall love the seaside," he said. "There will be bathing machines and wooden spades, and ever so much sand to dig in."

"But how do you know?" asked the older of the girls.

"Grandmother took me one summer," said the boy. "We stayed at a lodging house near the bandstand, and at night we could hear the music and the sound of the waves on the shingle through the open window."

"Goodness!" exclaimed Cratchit, with a flash of recognition.

"I think it must be young Tim, my grandson. But how he's grown. He can't have gotten so tall just since Christmas."

"These are the shadows of things yet to come," said Scrooge. "Our guide has a special talent for revealing such things," he added, giving a nod in the direction of the ghost, who towered behind them.

"Was Grandfather there?" asked the girl who had spoken before.

"Goodness, no," laughed Tim. "Christmas morning—that's all Grandfather is good for. You shan't catch him making merry on the beach when there's work to be done in that office of his."

"What does Grandfather do in his office, anyway?" asked the girl.

"Something to do with money and numbers," said Tim sagely. "You're too young to understand."

"It sounds dreadfully dull," said his sister. "When I'm grown I shall play at the seaside with my grandchildren instead of working in a dingy old office."

"So shall I," said Tim forcefully.

"Which one is Grandfather?" asked the younger girl, speaking for the first time since finishing her cake.

"The one who brings the lovely presents on Christmas and laughs at the table with the grown-ups," said Tim.

"I should prefer a playmate all the year round to the love-liest present at Christmas," said the young girl.

"That's why we have two grandfathers," laughed Tim. "One to bring presents and one to be our friend!"

"But the young Mrs. Cratchit's father doesn't bring lovely presents," protested Cratchit.

"Of course he doesn't," said Scrooge. "You do."

"Do you mean to say," began Cratchit, but he stopped in midsentence as he realised the full import of the conversation between his grandson and his future granddaughters.

A chill seemed to overtake the room, and the figures of the children became like gauze, until they dissolved away altogether and the two men found themselves again on a dim street with the silent Spirit. Neither Scrooge nor Cratchit recognised their surroundings as any part of London, but they followed the ghost through a tall stone arch into a courtyard from which a dozen or so doors led into the surrounding buildings.

Through one of these doors the trio somehow passed, and they soon found themselves in a tiny room where a single boy might conduct his studies. In this space, with its wooden desk, stool, and reading chair and by the light of a single lamp, six young men sprawled, lounged, lay, sat, and leaned. Somehow, though neither of the men could explain how afterwards,

Scrooge, Cratchit, and the deathly Spirit found space to stand amongst the boys.

Outside, the snow was piled high and fell so thickly that the building opposite was barely visible. The wind rattled the windowpanes, but a fire leapt merrily in the grate and its cheeriness seemed to have lured the boys to this particular study.

"The worst thing about being trapped here for Christmas by the snow," said a boy on whose knee an open (and ignored) book on Euclid perched precariously, "is that I will miss seeing my grandfather. He's a right jolly bloke and fancies himself a sort of Father Christmas. He came to live at the country house when I was six, and he's a great one for riding. Taught me everything I know about horses."

"It's true," said another, who sat on the windowsill, his scrawny legs dangling almost to the floor. "I've been riding with Cartwright's grandfather myself. He took me on my first hunt."

"I remember it well," said the boy who was evidently Cartwright. "Heathcote here got lost in the woods on the far side of the lake, and Grandfather had a devil of a time tracking him down." This revelation led to a general outburst of laughter at Heathcote's expense, but the boy in question laughed as hard as any of his cohorts.

"But he did track me down," said Heathcote at last, "and

he walked me all the way back to the lodge. I shall not forget his kindness."

"I remember my grandfather teaching me draughts in the study at Alwood House," said a boy who was propped up in the doorframe. "He would play with me for hours and I thought I was ever so clever because I always won. It wasn't until I met an old man in the lane one day that I learned that Grandfather hadn't lost a game of draughts in the pub for six years."

"Mine read to me," said the boy who lay on the floor, "before he died." A stillness fell over the room at the mention of death, and Bob Cratchit eyed the dark Spirit, who lurked in the corner. "He read me *Jane Eyre* and *Silas Marner*, and I shall never forget, the last year he was with us, he sat with me by the fire on Christmas Eve and read *The Rose and the Ring*. He did the most marvellous voices, and I remember that just as Grandfather was reading the last lines of the story, the old clock struck midnight. I thought Mother and Father would be horrified if they knew how late we had stayed up."

"What about you, Cratchit?" said the boy at the desk, who seemed to be the host.

A gangly youth who sat on the floor with his back against the wall stared at his boots with a stern expression for several seconds before answering. "Well, I suppose the best thing my grandfather ever did was send me to this school."

"Moneybags, eh?" said Cartwright.

"It's all very well," said Cratchit. "I mean, I certainly can't complain about the presents and the money for school, but it should have been nice to actually see the old man once in a while." And then Cratchit tossed his head back and laughed a short scoffing laugh. "It's a pity about your grandfather, Grimes, but be glad you knew him. I'm not sure I should recognise my grandfather if I passed him in the street. Nor he me."

"Enough of this torture!" said Bob Cratchit, averting his eyes from his grandson's face. "Show me no more of these shadows! I shall take the day off tomorrow, Mr. Scrooge, I promise. I shall take as many days off as you will give me, if only you tell me that there is some hope for changing these shadows. Is there hope? Is there? Are these the shadows of the things that will be, or are they shadows of things that may be, only?"

But neither Scrooge nor the Spirit answered the question, and the boys went on talking and comforting poor Grimes on the loss of his grandfather, but their voices faded away until they sounded as the lowing of cattle on a distant hill on a summer's day, and then the room itself melted from before their eyes and the air around them grew cold as ice and they stood on a city street before the open doors of a parish church. On the opposite corner stood two dark figures, huddled in conversation as the wind whipped around their ankles. Scrooge pushed Cratchit forward, and Cratchit slowly ventured to cross the street, but the spectre that accompanied them remained at the doorway of the church, unseen by the vicar who peered out from within, then checked his watch before disappearing back into that holy place.

Cratchit approached the two figures in the street and saw in one a reflection of his own face. "Is this me?" he asked, turning to Scrooge. But Scrooge, whose face seemed to have taken on the quality Cratchit would have expected in the visage of the spectre, if the spectre ever showed itself, only raised his hand and pointed to the pair. Cratchit took a step closer and listened.

"And why should I come to the funeral?" said the man whose face was hidden from Cratchit. He could tell from the voice that this was the younger of the two men, and that he was in the midst of a heated argument. "Did the old man ever come anywhere for me?"

"He came to the church when you were christened and again when you were married. It's only right that you see him to a Christian burial."

"Humbug. I don't suppose he would have even come to the wedding if Uncle Scrooge hadn't insisted on closing the office for the day. Of course I went to Scrooge's funeral, for he showed me no end of kindnesses from my earliest days. Scrooge was my grandfather, not the man lying in that church."

"Your grandfather only worked so hard because he loved his family," said the older man. "Think of all the things he made possible—your school, the university, your trip to the Continent. Do you think you could have had those things without him?"

"Funerals are for mourning," said the young man, "and we mourn those we know. It is true that my grandfather was a great benefactor and for that I suppose I should and shall be grateful, but I did not know him. I shall come to the reading of the will, for that's what he would have wanted. But he'd know me for a hypocrite if I mourned him at a funeral. He was content to visit me only once a year—on Christmas—surely he'll understand if I wish to forego this visit."

The young man turned and marched down the road, leaning into the cold wind and disappearing around the corner. When he was out of sight, the older man trudged across the street to the church door, paused for a moment, gazing down the street, then ducked into the church. Scrooge stood watching the spot where the young man had disappeared (for to him as well as to Cratchit, these shadows of the future were revelations), until he realised that Cratchit had followed the older man across the street and was even now peering in the door of the church to the gloom within.

Cratchit seemed about to step into the nave, when a hand from within pushed the door slowly shut, and Scrooge's partner was left staring at the weathered wood a few inches in front of him. In another instant he rounded on the Spirit, who still lurked nearby, and charged him in a fury, tears coursing down his face.

"Answer me, Spirit—am I the man who lies dead in that church? Am I?"

The finger pointed from the church to him, and back again.

"No, Spirit! Oh, no, no!"

The finger still was there. And before the finger, in the space between the spectre and the two men, there appeared a rapid series of pictures—whether they were visions shared by Scrooge and Cratchit or some conjuring of the spectre, the men never knew, but the images appeared as if a magic lantern were focused on some invisible wall, shifting from one slide to the next with dizzying speed. Scrooge knew not what he saw, but Cratchit recognised all his children and their families, all similarly neglected by their father or grandfather. And then the fashions changed, and Cratchit knew that he was peering into future generations of his family, and he saw in the faces of those whose parents and grandparents were yet unborn a coldness that came, he knew all too well, from a lifetime too focused upon labour. His blood ran through his veins like the icy water of the Thames at Christmas as he saw his own neglect spinning out across generation after generation, and whilst the clothing and the surroundings of all those future Cratchits who took their turns in the frigid night air told of their worldly riches, there was always within their eyes something lacking—and Cratchit recoiled in horror as the heavy truth fell upon him. His descendants in their scores and hundreds understood the ways of wealth and money and even of philanthropy, but their hearts lacked the true wealth of love, of family, of Christmas joy, which, he now saw, might have been theirs all the year round.

"Spirit!" he cried, tightly clutching at its robe. "Hear me! I am not the man I was. I will not be the man I must have been but for this intercourse. Why show me this, if I am past all hope?" Cratchit fell to his knees before the Spirit, and his sobs echoed in the empty street.

Scrooge, who knew full well the terror that came from the vision of one's own death—a vision of all the lost chances and wasted opportunities of a lifetime pressed upon a soul in a single moment—stepped forward to lay a hand on his partner's shoulder and stooped to whisper into Cratchit's ear, "All is not lost. These are but shadows; the child is but a babe. There is no need to see him only on Christmas Day."

Though he did not turn his face away from the Spirit or

release his grip on those long black robes, Cratchit seemed to hear Scrooge, for he raised his face to where the spectre's eyes ought to have been and said, "I will honour Christmas in my heart and try to keep it all the year. I will be like brother and father and friend and teacher to the boy and to his sisters and to all my grandchildren, if you will but tell me that these shadows will be erased!" But as Cratchit pulled on the robes, the spectre pulled back, and each, for a moment, tugged with such strength that Scrooge thought the fabric must be rent asunder and he averted his eyes, for he had no wish to have the spectre's true form revealed. But he needn't have feared, for as Cratchit gave a final jerk to the ghostly garment, he was pulling on nothing more supernatural than the curtains at his own window, and Scrooge stood not in a cold empty street but by the open door, where the warm breath of a summer morning was beginning to blow into the room.

✷

The End of It

S crooge had but few moments to observe the change that overcame his partner as Cratchit looked around the room and his eye fell on the blue paper cover of the monthly install-ment of the novel he had been reading a lifetime ago, it seemed. Though tears still dampened his cheeks and his breath came in choking sobs, he nonetheless realised the import of where that booklet lay—not on the floor, where it had fallen when he had been startled by Scrooge's arrival, but on the table by his chair, where it had lain *before* he had begun his night's reading. Cratchit rounded on Scrooge, a smile breaking across his face.

"It is not thrown down!" cried Cratchit, pointing a shak-ing finger towards the table. "It is not thrown down upon the hearthrug." With this, he snatched the booklet off the table and clutched it in his hand with a violence that would likely have displeased the author. "It is here!" he cried, shaking the booklet at Scrooge. "I am here; the shadows of the things that would have been may be dispelled. They *will* be. I *know* they will!"

But even as Cratchit's tears of terror and remorse turned to tears of joy and resolve, Scrooge felt himself drifting away from the scene and all that had lain before him. The threadbare chair, the table bearing the extinguished lamp, the kitchen awaiting the arrival of Mrs. Cratchit, and the trembling figure on the floor faded away and the sound of Cratchit's sobs became the ticking of the clock on Scrooge's own chimneypiece. The same warm air drifted in at Scrooge's window, but as he threw up the sash and stuck his head out into the London morning, the old man found that the weather had broken, and the oppressive humidity of yesterday had given way to crisp, clean air, warmed by the summer sun but wrapped in the promise of cool autumn days to come.

"Hallo!" he shouted at a boy who made his way along the street below. "Can you tell me what day it is?"

The boy, who was not previously acquainted with Scrooge's eccentricities, cast a puzzled look upwards and, seeing no harm in the old man, shouted back, "Twenty-third of June, sir."

"They've done it again!" cried Scrooge with glee. "The

spirits have done it all in one night. They can do anything they like. Of course they can. Of course they can."

You may never have seen such a thing as a man who has passed four score years on this earth dancing a jig in his nightshirt on a summer morning, but I assure you it is a sight well worth seeing, and one that would have provided you with plentiful laughter had you been in Scrooge's apartment that morning to see it. And had you been there, you might also have understood the expression "in a twinkling," for Scrooge's eyes never stopped twinkling in anticipation of the visits he planned to pay that morning.

As he hurried through the crowded morning streets after making himself presentable, even those who knew Scrooge well and were accustomed to his unseasonable greetings thought they detected an extra degree of enthusiasm in his bellows of "Merry Christmas!" and "Happy New Year!" He carried his walking stick only so he could swing it with gusto, wore a hat solely that he might tip it at every passing lady, patted the head of every child who ventured within his reach (and a few who tried, but failed, to give him a wide enough berth), and stuck his head in every shop he passed to remark on the fineness of the day, the fineness of the meat (or books, or pastries, or whatever was on offer), and the fineness of Christmas, which, by the way, he hoped would be merry for all.

Scrooge's first stop was Whitehall, where he expected to find his nephew perched on his stool and hard at work. However, though the morning had advanced past the point at which civil servants can generally be counted upon to be adding up columns of numbers for the good of England, Freddie's stool stood empty.

"Haven't you heard?" asked the clerk on the adjacent stool. "He talked as if it were all your idea."

After wishing the fellow the merriest of Christmases, Scrooge enquired as to the nature of the idea attributed to him.

"Freddie's decided to run for Parliament," said the clerk. "There were some in the office who found it quite a shock, I don't mind telling you; but many of us wondered what took him so long. I always knew he could do it."

"Do what?" asked Freddie with a scowl, for he had just arrived at the door.

"Ah, there you are, nephew," said Scrooge. "I had hoped I might have a chat with you this morning."

"A chat?" replied Freddie sternly. "I should think there are more important things in this world than chatting with one's uncle."

"And what might those be?" asked Scrooge, concerned with this unexpected standoffishness in his nephew's demeanour.

"Why, wishing him a Merry Christmas, for a start!" cried

Freddie, breaking into a smile and throwing his arms round his uncle. "And a Happy New Year, uncle, for it is a new year for me. A new year and a new life all beginning today, thanks to you." Freddie pulled his uncle by the sleeve into a corner of the room hidden from the other clerk by a filing cabinet and whispered, "All those years ago, when you told us about being visited by those spirits—we all thought you'd gone a bit potty, you know. Most of the family still think so, though they'd never say it to your face. But, oh, uncle! What a night! What a revelation! I never understood before now." And unable to think of what to say next, he again embraced his uncle with another "Merry Christmas," hearty enough to be heard clearly by the clerk who put so much faith in Freddie's future.

If Scrooge had hoped to chat with his nephew, he found the chat rather one-sided, for it was nigh on impossible for him to squeeze a word into Freddie's unstoppable torrent of excitement. Like the surf in a winter storm came Freddie's ideas, one after the other, without a moment to catch one's breath in between whiles. He would propose this and he would do something about that; he had a plan for one problem and an idea about another. If Freddie had been made dictator of the empire at that very moment, I daresay the world would have been a much better place in a fortnight, but Scrooge

knew that even as a lowly backbencher Freddie could, and
would, do much good, and he might well rise through the
ranks to higher and more influential posts as the years went
by. He smiled as Freddie spoke, but after a time Scrooge did
not hear every word his nephew said, for he thought he might
hear, faintly on the wind, another sound—the sound of chains
falling to the ground, link by link. If Freddie accomplished
one-twentieth of what he set for himself, Marley would certainly be a free man.

It took no small effort for Scrooge to extricate himself from
the conversation, and it was only when Freddie realised that
he was late for a meeting with a gentleman likely to back his
candidacy that Scrooge was able to bid his nephew farewell
and press on to his next destination.

Up Whitehall to Trafalgar, up the Strand and Fleet Street
and into the City strode Scrooge, whilst a sea of Londoners
parted in front of him, none quite sure how to respond to his
wishes for a Merry Christmas. When he arrived at the bank,
his request to see the Messrs. Pleasant and Portly was met
with a blank stare by the clerk in the cage. Laughing at his
own foolishness, Scrooge enquired after the bankers again,
this time using their proper names, which he had somehow
managed to remember (when he thought it over afterwards,

he suspected that Marley, who surely would have known, had whispered the names in his ear).

The clerk informed him that the two bankers he sought were engaged in a highly important conference with a highly important client and were not to be disturbed under any circumstances unless they were to receive a visit from one Ebenezer Scrooge.

"But I am Ebenezer Scrooge," he said, laughing.

"He is, you know," said the clerk in the next cage with a roll of his eyes. "Though I'm surprised he hasn't yet wished you a Merry Christmas, it being June."

The first clerk, who was evidently new to the position, did not think Scrooge looked the sort of man for whom one ought to interrupt a highly important conference, but since two newly arrived customers were even then greeting Scrooge by name and being wished a Merry Christmas, there seemed to be no doubt about his identity, so the clerk led him away down a long narrow corridor and through a series of heavy oak doors until they arrived in a dim and stuffy anteroom.

"One moment, please," whispered the clerk, who proceeded to stand by the largest oak door they had yet encountered for nearly a minute before he ventured a timid knock. This effort was met with utter silence.

"I'm sorry," whispered the clerk. "Perhaps they didn't want to be disturbed after all."

"Nonsense!" cried Scrooge, elbowing his way past the clerk and banging on the door with the handle of his walking stick. Before the clerk could restrain him, the door opened slightly and the scowling face of Mr. Portly appeared.

"I'm sorry, sir," muttered the clerk, "I tried to . . ." But what he tried to do Mr. Portly never discovered, for as soon as Portly saw Scrooge, he swung the door open and grinned with delight.

"Mr. Scrooge, what a pleasure! What a delight. We'd no idea you would honour us so soon with a visit." The befuddled clerk took this opportunity to make his exit, and Mr. Portly grabbed Scrooge by the hand and, shaking vigourously, pulled him into the inner sanctum in which the highly important conference was taking place.

The room might easily have contained Bob Cratchit's entire house; Freddie's family might have comfortably lounged in the fireplace; the table was as large as the stage of a West End theatre; and the woman who sat at the table (next to Mr. Pleasant, who now jumped from his seat to greet Scrooge by shaking the hand not claimed by Mr. Portly) wore a diamond ring that might, if pawned, have covered the weekly deposits in the bank with change left over for Sunday dinner.

"We're so pleased you've joined us, Mr. Scrooge," said Mr. Pleasant, apparently loath to release Scrooge's hand until the old man was comfortably seated in a chair large enough that it might accommodate (and the thought occurred to all three men at once) the Ghost of Christmas Present.

"This is Mr. Scrooge," said Mr. Portly, turning to the lady, who sat patiently at the far end of the table.

"Yes," added Mr. Pleasant, as if she might not have heard (and she was, indeed, quite far away), "this is Mr. Scrooge."

"It's a pleasure to meet you, Mr. Scrooge," said the lady, with a slight nod of her head.

Scrooge was on his feet again as soon as Messrs. Pleasant and Portly dropped his hands, and he skipped around the table to where the lady sat so that he might offer a proper greeting. Taking a deep bow, he said, "The pleasure is all mine," and then, looking her straight in her deep-set blue eyes, he added, "And may I take the opportunity of wishing you a very Merry Christmas."

The woman's face, which had remained unmoved up to this point, now showed the slightest flicker of what might have been delight or amusement or both, and she said in a soft voice, "I thank you, sir, and a Happy New Year to you and your family. Mrs. Aurelia Burnett Crosse at your service."

"Ebenezer Scrooge at yours. I do hope I'm not interrupting."

"On the contrary, sir," said Mrs. Crosse, "we were only just bemoaning your absence. Your arrival could not have been more propitious."

"Mrs. Crosse is one of our very best clients," said Mr. Portly.

"One of their very wealthiest clients, he means," said Mrs. Crosse with a laugh. "I'm afraid, Mr. Scrooge, you'll find me quite inept when it comes to the old stricture against talking about money. I have quite a lot of it, and, as I'm sure your friends here will tell you, there are days on which I talk of little else."

"You see, Mr. Scrooge," said Mr. Pleasant excitedly, "after our . . ."

"Our adventure last night," continued Mr. Portly.

"Yes," said Mr. Pleasant. "After our adventure, we decided we would find a way to help some of those people we met and to . . ."

"To cover some of your cheques!" cried Mr. Portly.

"Exactly," said Mr. Pleasant. "To cover some of your cheques."

"And there is no one in London more suited to the task of covering cheques than myself," said Mrs. Crosse.

"So you see," said Mr. Portly, "we're forming a little society."

"The Scrooge Society," said Mr. Pleasant.

"Yes, the Scrooge Society," continued Mr. Portly. "We've asked a few of our best clients."

"Your wealthiest clients," said Mrs. Crosse with a twinkle in her eye.

"As you put it," said Mr. Portly, "our wealthiest clients. We've asked them to join this society and to start a fund to be used for the relief of distress."

"With the funds to be dispensed at the sole discretion of Mr. Ebenezer Scrooge!" cried Mr. Pleasant.

"And when I leave, Mr. Scrooge, you shall have a thousand pounds at your disposal, so you'd best get to work, because I assure you there is more where that came from."

Scrooge could not hide his delight, and there followed a period of hand shaking and backslapping and Merry Christ-masing such as had not been seen in that hallowed chamber for many a year (if, in fact, the eyes of the portrait above the chimneypiece had ever witnessed such a display). Scrooge agreed to dine with Messrs. Pleasant and Portly the following day to discuss the details of how the charity they had insisted on naming in his honour would be administered. For the moment, though, he said that he must be going, as he had a rather important visit to pay.

It was past his usual luncheon time when Scrooge arrived

at his place of business, but earthly hunger had no effect on him that day. He was pleased to find the offices shut tight, and no sign that they had been occupied since the previous evening.

Scrooge's last visit of the day was brief. He shook no hands, slapped no backs, made no bows, and wished no one a merry anything. The street on which Timothy and Lucie Cratchit lived was, like their home, neat and modest. At two o'clock on a summer afternoon, it was empty of pedestrians, save for an old man in a colourful waistcoat strolling slowly away from the Cratchit home, a tear glistening in his eye. Scrooge had arrived at the Cratchits' only a few moments earlier and, peeping over the garden wall, had observed his partner, Bob, on his hands and knees in the garden doing a passable impression of a lion, whilst his grandson toddled towards him. Scrooge did not watch long enough to discover if little Tim was playing the role of big game hunter or lion tamer; he had seen enough to know that his work was done.

S crooge half-expected another visit from Marley that evening, and sat up reading for some hours (long enough to see the young boy in the novel become a young man) before he despaired of a visit from his friend. It was nearly autumn when Marley did return, a night with a bite in the air cold enough that Scrooge entertained thoughts of a closed window and a fire in the grate. If a spirit can be said to smile, on that night Marley did. His chain, he said, was considerably lighter thanks to Scrooge's machinations, and growing lighter every day. It was nearly four years before Marley paid his final visit, and on that occasion Scrooge's late partner, overcome with emotion, could only mumble a simple thanks for the rest that was, at last, about to come his way.

Cratchit continued to work hard, but he left the office after lunch every Tuesday and spent the afternoon with his grandson; Scrooge saw to it that Cratchit's income did not suffer for this indulgence. Tim always looked upon his grandfather with eyes full of love, and would consider the hours the two spent together amongst the happiest of his childhood. As Cratchit's life became blessed with additional grandchildren, he spent more time with them and less at the office, until Scrooge convinced his partner to take early retirement and to hand the reins of the business over to his son. From that day forward, not a day passed when Cratchit did not bless the life of some member of his increasing family with an act of kindness or a display of love, and it was said by those who knew him that he taught all the Cratchit grandchildren the true meaning of family and that they would doubtless carry this lesson forth in the world as they married and had children and grandchildren of their own.

Freddie did his best to be a great reformer, and though he never became prime minister, he did attain various positions of influence and he was often, behind closed doors, the initiator and driving force behind many of the social improvements in the ensuing two decades. In his retirement, he continued to administer the charity founded in honour of his uncle.

The Scrooge Society (which eventually included several members of Parliament in addition to Freddie) met for luncheon at the club of Messrs. Pleasant and Portly every Wednesday. Scrooge had wanted to change the name to the Wednesday Club, but the members insisted that the name reflect the role Mr. Scrooge had played in all their lives. These pages are too brief to enumerate all the good the society did as the years passed, but many a desperate Londoner had his life transformed by the generosity of its members, and though the money they gave away was not, strictly speaking, Scrooge's, they nonetheless depended on the old man's guidance. And Scrooge's understanding of the people of London, coupled with his genuine belief that they were, as his nephew had said so long ago, fellow passengers to the grave, always steered the society towards accomplishing true change in the lives of the people it touched.

Scrooge never stopped wandering the streets of London, looking for places where he might spread the spirit of Christmas and wishing the passersby a happy holiday. And though he preferred to be known as an eccentric old man rather than as a benefactor, Scrooge was not quite so anonymous as to have his deeds go wholly unrecognised. And so it was that, on occasion, whilst strolling down the Strand or when stopped before the window of a bookshop on Charing Cross Road, Scrooge would encounter some former beneficiary of his kindness, and that fortunate soul, be it man, woman, or child, would invariably greet him with a hearty, "God bless you, Mr. Scrooge," to which Scrooge would as invariably reply, "God bless *us*, every one."

The End

Afterword

The gratitude I feel for Charles Dickens extends far beyond the inspiration for (and some of the passages in) this little story. Although Dickens may have been overcredited in the early twentieth century for single-handedly both reviving the observance of Christmas and inventing our modern version of its celebration, he certainly played an important role in codifying many Christmas customs that remain in use to this day—from carol singing to tree decorating. As I look back on the Christmas celebrations of my childhood, I marvel at how much of what Christmas means to me comes from (or at the very least *through*) Mr. Dickens, and how much is rooted in the England of the early 1840s.

Our family was self-consciously English in our Christmas celebrations. We belonged to an Episcopal church, where we attended Christmas Eve services in the Anglican tradition. True to Mr. Dickens's call to make Christmas a time of generosity to those less fortunate, we brought presents to church for needy children. We had roast beef and Yorkshire pudding for Christmas dinner and one year my father and I scoured the city for plum pudding only to be disappointed when we arrived at the one grocery store that had said on the phone, yes they had some, to find nothing more British than purple Jell-O. We listened to Handel's *Messiah* and sang carols around the piano as my sister played, and of course, thanks in part to Prince Albert, who popularized the tradition in England around 1840, we decorated a Christmas tree.

Most of these traditions remain a part of my family's Christmas celebrations. My wife and I have, for almost twenty years, sung in the choir at St. Timothy's Episcopal Church in Winston-Salem, North Carolina. On Christmas Eve we often sing two services, culminating in the eleven o'clock mass, at which we take Communion a few minutes after midnight. We try to make Christmas a time of generosity to others and of love and gratitude expressed to members of our own family.

We also send Christmas cards to distant friends and family—a tradition started by Sir Henry Cole in England in 1843, the same year that *A Christmas Carol* was published. Years ago a friend of mine who is an antiquarian bookseller had a copy of the first-ever Christmas card for sale and showed it to me—it pictures a large family eating and drinking together. Even the small children receive a sip of wine, and I was reminded of the tiny cordial glass of wine that would sit at my place at Christmas dinner when I was a child. On either

side of this central, colored image are two uncolored scenes—
one showing a man distributing bread to the poor and another
showing a woman draping a cloak over a cold mother with a
baby. It was wonderful to see in this card the two ideas that
we hold closest at Christmastime (and that Dickens promotes
in his famous story): feasting and celebration with family, and
care for and generosity to others.

In 2003, my wife, daughter, and I spent Christmas in
England. My daughter's high school glee club was scheduled
to sing in London the week after Christmas, so we decided
to go a few days early. I was, at the time, teaching a seventh-
grade English class for a few months while a friend was on
maternity leave. I had only one student in my study hall—an
independent-minded young man to whom I carefully intro-
duced Monty Python as an extension of our study of Arthurian
legends. Each day, after I had read to him a scene (edited for
seventh-grade ears) from *Monty Python and the Holy Grail*, he
would get to work on his assignments and I would pull out a
new project of my own. Since we were planning on Christmas
in England I had been thinking a lot about English Christmas
celebrations in general and about Charles Dickens in particular, so I thought I would try my hand at writing a sequel to
A Christmas Carol. In the context of King Arthur and Monty
Python, I had had a conversation with my student about

parody, so I decided to begin my story with a parody of Dickens's opening passage.

What if, I wondered, Ebenezer Scrooge had, following his
conversion at the end of *A Christmas Carol*, embraced Christmas with the same fervor with which he had previously rejected
it? So I made both Scrooge and the day on which the story
was set the antithesis of what they had been in *A Christmas
Carol* and waited to see where the old man (for he must be in
his eighties by now) would take me.

My family and I arrived in England a few days before
Christmas and had a light schedule—a jaunt down to the
coast, where we walked atop the chalk cliffs of Beachy Head,
and a relaxed couple of days in a luxurious country hotel in
Kent, which my wife, Janice, and I had discovered a few years
earlier when we were on a pilgrims' walk from Rochester to
Canterbury. At this hotel that had once been a country home
I slid into a plush armchair in front of a roaring fire flanked
by Christmas trees and worked on my story about Ebenezer
Scrooge—what better place to write? Perhaps only the place
where I wrote on Christmas Eve. We could not resist the
opportunity to attend the Christmas Eve service at Canterbury
Cathedral, presided over by the Archbishop of Canterbury
himself. We arrived early to claim a seat in the choir so we
could see the service of lessons and carols unfold. With nearly

an hour before the service started, I pulled out my notebook and continued my tale of Mr. Scrooge until I heard, with perfect clarity in the massive cathedral's ringing acoustics, the voice of a boy soprano singing "Once in Royal David's City" at the far end of the nave.

On Christmas morning we traveled into London to spend the day with friends. Later in the week, after we had heard the glee club sing in both sacred and secular settings, we took the train out to the little village of Kingham to spend New Year's Eve with more of our dear English friends. Throughout the week, in hotel rooms, on the train, and in a cozy drawing room in Kingham, I continued to work on Scrooge's story. I did not have a laptop at the time, so much of the first draft was written in longhand—but that seemed appropriate. Dickens, of course, had written all of his Christmas stories in longhand.

When we returned home I began burrowing through Dickens's writings, looking for descriptions of some of the places I wanted Scrooge to visit. Dickens had a great concern for social welfare, and I wanted that concern to be manifest in my story.

For a couple of months in 2004, I thought *The Further Adventures of Ebenezer Scrooge* would be my breakthrough book. I found an agent who liked it, he sent it to a few publishers, but ultimately no one bought it, the agent drifted away, and the book sat in a drawer (or at least the metaphorical drawer that comprises a computer file) for more than a decade.

In the meantime, I did have a breakthrough. In 2011, I signed a contract with Penguin for the publication of my novel *The Bookman's Tale.* This led to a close working and personal relationship with the wonderful Kathryn Court, president of Penguin Books and my indefatigable editor. Kathryn encouraged me to get straight to work on my second novel, and *First Impressions: A Novel of Old Books, Unexpected Love, and Jane Austen* was published in 2014, following the gratifying success of *The Bookman's Tale,* which had been published the previous year. In Kathryn's office one morning, after we had looked at the proposed dust jacket design for *First Impressions,* she and I had a talk about what might be next. We discussed several possible new projects, and just before I left I mentioned that I did have a Christmas story, one inspired by Dickens, already finished. Kathryn was immediately intrigued, and because I was busy editing *First Impressions,* I sent my agent a copy of the manuscript without even reading over it. I had not taken a close look (or even a perfunctory look) in many years, and I wasn't sure what to expect, so I was pleased to hear that Kathryn loved the story. I was equally pleased to find, when I did have a chance to reread it, that I did, too.

The book has a multilayered nostalgia for me—not only does it take me back to childhood Christmases and to my earliest encounters with Charles Dickens; it also, because of its long road to publication, reminds me of those lovely couple of months, now almost twelve years ago, when I was writing the first draft.

Astute readers will recognize many passages in *The Further Adventures of Ebenezer Scrooge* that come from works by Charles Dickens. His immortal 1843 book, *A Christmas Carol in Prose: Being a Ghost Story of Christmas*, is, of course, the major source and inspiration and I have taken the liberty of paraphrasing, parodying, and plagiarizing passages from that classic story. I wanted Scrooge's social concerns to reflect those of Mr. Dickens, and so some of the accounts of the less fortunate in Victorian London are taken directly from his works, including the descriptions of London slums from *Bleak House* (1853), an asylum from "A Curious Dance Round a Curious Tree" (*Household Words*, 1852), London rookeries from "Gin Shops" (*Evening Chronicle*, 1835), and debtors' prison from *Little Dorrit* (1857). The description of Scrooge's Christmas tree comes from Dickens's story "A Christmas Tree" (*Household Words*, 1850). And of course *David Copperfield* (1850) is not only the book that Scrooge reads in his lodgings; it is also the source of the scene in Murdstone and Grinby's, the warehouse Freddie visits.

Over the past three years, I have come to know many of my readers and I have often been touched and humbled by their responses to my work. I hope that you, as one of those readers, will look on this little book as my Christmas card to you, and with it my wish for you is that the spirit of Christmas may be with you always. May God bless you, every one.

Charlie Lovett
CHRISTMAS 2014

Acknowledgments

Thanks are due to the late Bill Carr for introducing me to the works of Charles Dickens; to Alex Reber, who encouraged me during the writing process, in spite of being a seventh grader at the time; to my colleagues at Summit School; and to our British friends who fed, housed, and celebrated with us over the Christmas holidays of 2003—Mark and Catherine Richards and Chris and Delphie Stockwell. I am, of course, deeply indebted to the works of the aforementioned Mr. Dickens. I am grateful for the support and enthusiasm of David Gernert and Anna Worrall at the Gernert Company and to my incredible team at Penguin, which includes but is not limited to Lindsey Schwoeri, Rebecca Lang, Annie Harris, and the remarkable Kathryn Court. Douglas Smith has created illustrations that perfectly capture the spirit and era of the text, and for that I am most grateful. Finally, to my loving and supportive family—I could not be more lucky than to have Lucy, Jordan, and Janice in my life.